Grandmother Came from Dworitz

© 1969, Ethel Vineberg

Published in Canada by Tundra Books, Montreal, Quebec H3G 1R4

Published in the United States by Tundra Books of Northern New York, Plattsburgh, N.Y. 12901

First edition 1969
French edition, *L'aïeule qui venait de Dworitz* 1969
First paperback edition 1978
Second paperback edition 1987

Canadian Cataloguing in Publication Data
Vineberg, Ethel
  Grandmother came from Dworitz

ISBN 0-88776-195-X

1. Jews – Canada – Biography – Juvenile literature. 2. Jews – Poland – Biography – Juvenile literature. I. Briansky, Rita II. Title.

FC106.J5V56 1987 j971'.004924022 C87-090065-X F1035.J5V56 1987

Printed in Canada

For My Grandchildren

Tamar, Lisa, David and Stephen

Grandmother Came from Dworitz

A Jewish love story

by Ethel Vineberg
illustrated by Rita Briansky

Tundra Books

In Eastern Europe, the Jews lived in small towns or villages known as *shtetl*

Foreword

I write this because I am the link between the old country and the new. I was born here, but my mother came from Europe. I shall tell you stories she told me and that her mother told her of a way of life that no longer exists. Wars and revolutions have changed it.

I begin with a little history so that you may understand my ancestors.

Historians tell us that after the destruction of the Temple in Jerusalem two thousand years ago, Jews entered Europe from Asia. Many settled in Western Europe and Germany. After the Crusades in the eleventh century, some Jews fled to Poland and settled there as traders. They were welcomed by the rulers of Poland who needed people to develop commerce and industry. As a result, large numbers of Jews followed from Germany. Their language came to be called Yiddish – it was a mixture of German, Polish and Hebrew.

The Kingdom of Poland was a small country bordering on three great powers. It was invaded many times and was completely conquered in 1795. Its land was divided among Russia, Prussia and Austria. Russia received as her share of the plunder the provinces of Vilna, Grodno and Minsk, and with this land came most of her Jewish population.

The Jewish people lived apart. They spoke only Yiddish and had little contact with the rest of the population, except in trade. They had their own schools. An elementary school was called a *cheder* and all boys from the age of six to thirteen had to attend; indeed, many started at an earlier age. On a boy's first day in school his father carried him through the door and gave him to the care of the teacher who would now take charge during all school hours. Small boys could be kept studying eight to twelve hours a day. Many tiny scholars, entering early and leaving late, never saw the sunshine and were always pale and wan. Time for play was not thought necessary to their well-being.

They studied the Bible in the original Hebrew, along with a translation in Yiddish. In a few *chedorim* Hebrew grammar and arithmetic were also taught; this depended on the ability of the teacher. Any man who knew enough to be an elementary school teacher or *malammed* was allowed to open a *cheder* for boys in his own home, and he was paid by the father of each pupil. Schools for orphans and the very poor were paid for by the Jewish community. In any disagreement among Jews, their own rabbis acted as judges.

There was always a tailor, a shoemaker, a baker and, sometimes, a tavern keeper in even the smallest village. There might be a storekeeper but most people traded in the marketplace.

Women often carried on business while their husbands studied in the synagogue. The synagogue

was the center of their life and they looked forward all
week to Saturday, the Sabbath. On Friday homes
were cleaned, all was made ready for the Sabbath
meal and in the late afternoon everyone went to the
crude bathhouses, one for the women and one for the
men, where they bathed and changed into their
Sabbath clothing. At sundown services began in the
synagogue.

The Saturday midday meal was always the best one of
the week. Strangers attending the synagogue service
and poor students were invited to a home for this
meal, and no family was ever allowed to go hungry if
the rabbi knew of their problem.

This all sounds pleasant enough, but life was not easy.

The Russian government was very hard on the Jews. They were allowed to live only in the three provinces that had formerly belonged to Poland, and this land came to be known as the Pale of Settlement. Jews could live or work in other parts of Russia only by special permission. Permits to travel were given by the government to a very few who had business outside the Pale.

Jews were not allowed to own land. They lived in small towns and villages, and most of them were poor. Very few Jews spoke Russian or Polish. The Russian government found this very awkward when dealing with Jews; they therefore chose one man in each town or village to act as spokesman for his fellow Jews. This man was one who had learned to speak Russian and who could be accepted as a leader by his people. The man chosen did not always have an easy time; he could easily displease both the Russians *and* the Jews, especially in such matters as taxes and army service.

My great-grandfather held this difficult position.

Water had to be brought from well or river for all the cooking and washing

I
Lechovitch

Hirsch Mishkofsky was born about 1820 in
Lechovitch, Minsk Gabernia. He was a tall, handsome
man with blond hair and blue eyes. He spoke Russian,
was very dignified and became a natural leader of his
people. His business was an inn and post station
where travelers changed horses. In those days people
traveled only on horseback or by post chaise, and they
had to change horses often. Roads were poor and
there were no railways.

Mishkofsky was well-off for his time and place. In 1853
his wife, Mary Yudelevsky, gave birth to a daughter
after having borne three sons. The parents were very
pleased and called the welcome little girl Sarah Elca.
The baby was fair with blue eyes; she was plump,

healthy and a gay, fun-loving child. As she grew older, she always felt a little guilty at being happy, as this was a time when Jewish children were not supposed to be light in spirit.

Sarah Elca – like the other girls in the town – did not attend school. She was taught to sew and to read her prayer book in Hebrew. Years later in the village of Dworitz, she was the only woman who could read Hebrew and she led the women in prayer in the balcony of the little synagogue.

It was not thought a good idea to educate a girl. Education might keep her from having a happy marriage. Girls were supposed to follow the wishes of their parents until marriage. After marriage, they accepted the rule of their husbands. Education tends to make people ask questions and a girl with knowledge might grow dissatisfied with her narrow life. This was, of course, a general attitude in most of the world at that time, but the life of a Jewish maiden, or wife, was even more limited. Association with non-Jews was unthinkable, and the possibility of marriage outside their religion was as shocking as death. In fact, the latter was thought preferable.

Sarah Elca grew up in a comfortable brick house, although most of the houses in the town were of wood.

Sarah Elca did not attend school but was taught to sew at home

Her parents' home had several helpers to do the many hard chores. Someone had to chop the wood, carry it into the house, make the fires for heating and cooking. Water had to be brought from the well or the river for all the cooking and washing. Copper pots were used, and Friday morning the servant often started at 4:00 A.M. to polish them for the Sabbath.

A woman came in regularly to bake bread for the household and enough to give away to the poor. The cook was always the most important of the servants. In this family, she was a Jewish widow who knew how

to keep a strictly *kosher* kitchen. This was important because the Jewish religion has strict laws regarding food which must be observed. Anyone working in a Jewish kitchen had to be familiar with these laws.

Washing clothes was a very big task. It was not done as often as we do it today. Twice a year, four women came; there was much carrying of water and making of fires to heat the water. Soap which had been made at home was used. Vast quantities of clothing and bed linen were washed and dried in the open air. It took many people to keep the family comfortable and clean.

In 1868 Hirsch Mishkofsky suddenly realized that his daughter had grown up. He said to his wife, Mary: "Our Sarah Elca is already fifteen years of age. If we do not arrange a marriage for her, she may sit at home until she is nineteen years, God forbid."

This was a serious matter and Mary agreed that something must be done at once. In the family, there were now seven sons and two daughters; the youngest, Faigle, was only five years old.

Mishkofsky was an honored member of the synagogue in Lechovitch. He had been brought up in the tradition that an educated man, a man of the Talmud, is the most important of men. He felt that it would add prestige to his family if his daughter married a scholar, perhaps a future rabbi.

With this thought in mind, he set out on a journey by horse and carriage to Volozhin to visit the famous Yeshiva. A *yeshiva* is a college of higher Jewish learning where the Talmud, its commentaries, and other Jewish literature are studied. The Talmud is a book of Jewish civil and religious laws. Jewish problems or arguments were always settled according to the law of the Talmud. The instructors in *yeshivas* were learned rabbis.

The Volozhin Yeshiva had been founded in 1803 in the town of Volozhin, Vilna Gabernia. This school was the training ground of many of the best Jewish scholars of the early nineteenth century in Russia. It was modern for the time. Before then, Jewish youth were forbidden to study any subject which did not concern the Jewish religion and their past history. They wept for the destruction of the Temple in Jerusalem as though it had occurred yesterday. In the nineteenth century changes began to take place. Educated Jewish youth began to realize that there were horizons wider than their synagogue walls.

In 1868 the Volozhin Yeshiva was under the direction of the famous scholar, Rabbi Hirsch Lieb.

Hirsch Mishkofsky sets out for the Yeshiva in Volozhin to find a husband for his daughter

Mishkofsky arrived at the Yeshiva clad in a fur-lined coat. He looked prosperous and important. He had no difficulty getting an interview with Rabbi Lieb.

After formal greetings, the visitor gave Rabbi Lieb a description of his position in Lechovitch and said he wished to arrange a marriage for his daughter. He asked to be given the honor of meeting the Yeshiva's most brilliant student.

Rabbi Lieb stroked his beard and thought for a moment. He was impressed by the visitor's poise and manner. He knew of the standing of the Mishkofsky family. He realized that such a marriage would benefit a young student.

He sent for Mordche Zisel Shapiro.

Mordche Zisel was a boy of nineteen, slight in build, refined and delicate in appearance, with a gentle manner. He spoke easily and well, and Mishkofsky was favorably impressed.

Mordche Zisel was from Dworitz, Grodno Gabernia. His mother was now a widow and the young student was quite open to the idea of marriage and the chance to continue his studies for the rabbinate without further money worries.

The Volozhin Yeshiva was under the direction of the famous scholar,
Rabbi Hirsch Lieb

Mordche Zisel was a boy of nineteen, slight in build, refined and delicate in appearance

Plans were made for the young man to visit Lechovitch to be "heard" by the elders of the synagogue there.

Mishkofsky returned home. He reported to his wife, Mary, how pleased he had been with the student and of the plan made for the young man's visit.

A week later Mordche Zisel arrived in Lechovitch. He presented himself at Hirsch Mishkofsky's house and was taken into a sitting room to await the "elders."

There had been no thought of presenting him to Sarah Elca. At this time, no properly brought up Jewish girl was supposed to meet her husband until the day of the marriage.

Sarah Elca had heard her parents discussing the brilliant young man who might become her husband, and she was just as excited and curious as any girl of today would be. She made up her mind to see him.

She borrowed an apron from one of the servants and a kerchief for her head. She then walked timidly into the room where Mordche Zisel was waiting. She picked up a book as though that had been her errand and would have slipped quietly out again, having had her stolen glimpse. Mordche Zisel, however, was also curious and suspicious. He quickly asked her the name of the book she had taken. She replied shyly and left the room. Mordche Zisel smiled to himself for he knew he had seen his future bride. Servants in Russia in 1868 could not read.

Sarah Elca Mishkofsky and Mordche Zisel Shapiro were married in Lechovitch that same year. They had a large wedding and the bride was given a trousseau by her father with enough bed linen and clothing to last a lifetime. Sarah Elca's trousseau was well known to her children as many items were made over into clothes for them through the years.

The newly married couple lived with the bride's parents in Lechovitch. Mordche Zisel studied the Talmud and prepared for the rabbinate. He obtained *smichah*, a diploma permitting him to be a rabbi, from the Volozhin Yeshiva.

It was a period of changing attitudes and Mordche Zisel began to change. He wanted worldly, as well as

Sarah Elca, disguised as a servant, steals a look at her future husband

religious, knowledge; he studied mathematics, history and languages. Gradually, he gave up all desire to be a rabbi, much to his father-in-law's disappointment.

Mordche Zisel was a born student; he was quite willing to live year after year acquiring knowledge and carrying on endless discussions with other learned men. But Sarah Elca was not satisfied to live as a dependent of her parents. She longed for the dignity of her own establishment. When her husband decided that he would not be a rabbi, she insisted that he enter some other occupation.

He was now twenty-nine years old and she was twenty-five. She was always more energetic and more worldly than her studious and ascetic husband. She was not an intellectual, but a vital and lively person. She loved fun and good clothes. She would have enjoyed life in a larger society.

Mordche Zisel and Sarah Elca had lived for ten years supported by her father. The couple now had five children, four boys and one girl. The little girl was Nachama, and I shall tell you more about her later.

Dworitz had tall Orthodox and Roman Catholic churches and a small wooden synagogue

II
Dworitz

In 1878 Mordche Zisel and his wife and their five children moved to Dworitz. His mother had died, and he was now the owner of a one-story frame house in this village of about two hundred people. Lechovitch was a city by comparison: it had a population of six thousand.

Dworitz was a small village. There was an Orthodox Church for the Russians and a Roman Catholic Church for the Poles, and these two buildings were of brick and could be seen from any place in the village. The small Jewish synagogue was of wood, as were all the houses. Most of the buildings were one story.

The road through the village was muddy most of the

year; there were no sidewalks, not even wooden ones. There were no flowers or trees, and goats and chickens ran about freely.

The distance between Lechovitch and Dworitz was about thirty miles. The family traveled by horse and wagon and the trip took two days. The children were excited and interested in every new experience. Sarah Elca, although leaving security and some luxury in her parents' home, was nevertheless pleased at the prospect of a more independent life.

Clothing was always a problem; it was made over again and again. Sarah Elca's eldest son was given a fur-lined coat by his grandfather. When he outgrew it, the second son got it. But the sleeves were badly worn and had to be replaced by the tailor. Eventually, the third son came into possession of the coat, but the front now had to be replaced. Finally, when the fourth son took it over, there was nothing left of the original coat.

Though his own home was peaceful, Mordche Zisel was well aware of the tragedy of his people in Russia. The hard laws and lack of opportunity led to much poverty. "The Jewish Question" was a constant subject of talk in his household. Although he was modern enough to want more than a religious education, he remained orthodox in his religious observances and beliefs. His attitude toward the sufferings of the Jews was not a positive one demanding action, but the passive one of praying in the synagogue.

At Passover and at Rosh Hashanah (the Jewish New Year), Sarah Elca's father sent handsome gifts of woolen or satin material imported from Germany to be made into a suit or dress for his daughter. He also included a ruble (a Russian dollar) for each child, but this the children did not know until years later. Their mother, always short of money, used the rubles to pay the tailor.

The thirty-mile trip between Dworitz and Lechovitch took two days by horse and wagon

The family brought with them to Dworitz a young Jewish orphan to help with the children. This girl Rachel worked in the Shapiro home for eight years. She became a good cook and housekeeper.

Sarah Elca had been trained in the Jewish tradition of assuming responsibility for the weak, the sick, the widowed and the orphaned. When Rachel was twenty-two years of age, Sarah Elca said to her husband:

"Mordche Zisel, Rachel is of an age to be married. She is an orphan and has no one to look after her interests. We cannot take advantage of this, even though I find her a help and comfort to me. I would like to take her to my parents' home in Lechovitch and consult a marriage broker. I feel that it is our duty to arrange a marriage for her."

Mordche Zisel wholeheartedly agreed with his wife's plan.

Mistress and maid journeyed to Lechovitch. There Sarah Elca with her mother's help arranged a marriage for Rachel to a "good man." The two women gathered together a trousseau for the bride and arranged a suitable wedding.

Sarah Elca returned to Dworitz to bring her children to Rachel's wedding. As she dressed the children in their best clothes, she explained to them her philosophy.

"My children," she said, "when we attend the wedding of rich people, it does not matter how we dress, as long as we are neat, but when we go to the wedding of poor people, we must dress our very best, so that they will not think that we consider them unimportant."

When the family returned to Dworitz after the wedding, they missed the comfort of Rachel's help. They had other servant girls through the years, but no one ever quite took Rachel's place.

The Shapiro house contained a kitchen, storage places for food, a large room which was living and dining room, and bedrooms. The kitchen had a large square stove. An alcove in the wall over this stove contained a sort of bunk bed. Every Russian household had this bed over the stove. During the long Russian winter this was the most comfortable spot in the house. If there were old grandparents in the household, they were usually given this bed; if not, it was often used for the sick or delicate. The children loved to sleep in it and to play on it.

During the long Russian winter the alcove above the stove was the most comfortable spot in the house

Sarah Elca was quite satisfied with her home. In the main room she had a large dining table flanked by benches. There was a small table on which stood the brass samovar for serving tea. Mordche Zisel had a bookcase with double doors which could be locked. Books were very scarce and expensive in this age, and he was very careful of his small collection. When a man came to borrow a book from him, he took a small token from the borrower and locked it in the bookcase, to be given back when the book was returned.

In this tiny village, far from large cities, only Mordche Zisel and the two village priests received newspapers from the outside world. They often exchanged news with one another and discussed the happenings in the world.

In imperialist Russia where Jewish settlements were often attacked by mobs (this mob violence was called *pogroms*), this friendly relationship was probably a help to the Jewish population. The Jews of Dworitz never experienced this terror.

Mordche Zisel took on a job of bookkeeper and office manager of a large estate owned by his brother-in-law. In 1878 Jews were not allowed to own land in Russia, and certainly not a large estate. To explain how Mordche Zisel's brother-in-law came into his ownership, I must return for a moment to the history of Poland.

After Poland was divided in 1795, Russia found it difficult to keep her conquered Polish subjects under control. There were many revolts and, in 1863, a rebellion occurred.

Dworitz was on land belonging to a powerful Polish nobleman. The manor house and land adjoining the village were one of his smaller estates. When the Russians crushed the revolt of 1863, the nobleman came to this remote part of the country for shelter. Mordche Zisel's sister and brother-in-law kept him hidden until it was possible for him to escape from the country. He remained abroad until the Russians gave up looking for the rebel leaders. In gratitude, he then gave his protectors the estate near Dworitz for their lifetime. The nobleman came once every two years on a token visit.

The estate was about two miles from Dworitz. A beautiful road bordered by tall trees led onto it. Orchards of apples, pears, plums and cherries blossomed and bore fruit. Grain was grown in quantities; a mill ground the flour; a distillery made liquor from the rye. All kinds of vegetables were grown. Animals and fowl were raised and killed when necessary for food. Dairy products were plentiful.

Mordche Zisel's family was provided with food in ample quantities. The life of the family at home was easy and pleasant. Sarah Elca was concerned for those not so well-off. During the bad seasons when the peasants or poor Jews lacked daily bread, they could always get help from Sarah Elca.

Although food was plentiful, money was always scarce. Mordche Zisel received a small salary and this was spent almost entirely on his sons' education. The boys were educated first in private *chedorim*, and later at the Slonim and Mir Yeshivas.

Although land could not be registered in the name of a Jew, Mordche Zisel's brother-in-law ran the estate and drew the income from it. His family lived in a large stone house with very thick walls. The windows were set in so deeply that little Nachama could curl up very comfortably on the windowsills to read. The

A beautiful road bordered by tall trees led onto the estate of the exiled
Polish nobleman

house had polished floors and furniture that had been imported. A piano was brought from Paris for the only daughter of the family.

It was at this time that Hirsch Mishkofsky, Sarah Elca's father, left Russia to spend his declining years in Palestine near the site of the destroyed Temple. To die in the Holy Land and be buried in its sacred soil was the desperate desire of orthodox Jews. They lived in an alien and unfriendly world. In death they longed to return to their own land. Hirsch Mishkofsky is buried in Mea Shorim, the old cemetery in Jerusalem.

Mordche Zisel loved his daughter, Nachama, and she adored and revered him. In her eyes he could do no wrong. Indeed, she thought all fathers were special people. Years later in New York she greatly amused her uncle who was criticizing an acquaintance, by exclaiming: "How can you say such things about Mr. S. – after all, he is a *father*."

Mordche Zisel often took her with him traveling on business to neighboring towns. He talked to her as an adult, and thus she came to know of the Jewish problems in Russia. Although she did not attend school, a Jewish woman taught her sewing and embroidery and another taught her to read and write Yiddish. Mordche Zisel, himself, taught her Hebrew

and some Russian. He said to her: "I wish you to read
Tenach (the Bible), my daughter, but I also wish you
to read Tolstoy." The Russian Count Leo Tolstoy is –
like Shakespeare and Molière – a giant among the
world's writers. Toward the end of his life he dressed
as a peasant and worked beside his men on the land.

Mordche Zisel watched hopefully the feeble attempts
to reform the government made under Czar
Alexander II. When that monarch was assassinated in
1881, the Polish Roman Catholic priest tapped on the
window of the Shapiro home long after midnight to

tell him the terrible news. Mordche Zisel wept
bitterly, not because he loved Alexander but because
he feared the actions of the next czar. His fears were
well-founded.

Conditions in Russia were very bad. Those in power
were corrupt and incapable. The peasants were
oppressed and hungry. In order to turn their attention
away from their own hard lot, they were secretly
encouraged to attack the Jews. The pogroms that
followed started the great exodus of Jews to America.
In the next eight years, more than 200,000 Jews
emigrated from Russia to the United States and
Canada.

Nachama begged her father to allow her to go to
America. She did not want to sit at home and wait for
an arranged marriage. She was excited at the thought

of a country where everyone had the opportunity to study or work, where work was looked upon as an honorable way of life, even for a girl.

Her parents found it very hard to grant her permission to go. A steamship ticket sent by relatives in America lay in her father's bureau drawer for a whole year. Finally, with great reluctance and sorrow, and with the knowledge that conditions in Russia could only get worse, Mordche Zisel consented to let her travel to America in the care of a family he knew well.

The sight of the newly erected Statue of Liberty filled Nachama with joy after the long sea voyage

III
America

Nachama was small with fair skin, hazel eyes and softly waving brown hair. She was very happy to be going to America but before the long sea journey was over, she was sick and weary. She was not a good sailor and conditions on the ship were far from pleasant. The Jewish immigrants, accustomed to eating *kosher* food, ate only the food they had brought with them. This made their diet very sparse, especially toward the end of the voyage which lasted for several weeks.

The Statue of Liberty had been erected in New York Harbor in 1886. Six years later, in 1892, the sight of it with its promise of freedom filled Nachama with joy.

Nachama landed at Ellis Island, New York. One of her earliest memories was seeing a parade which commemorated the four hundredth anniversary of the discovery of America by Christopher Columbus in 1492.

She was received by her uncle Jacob Mishkin, her mother's brother, and was made very welcome in his home. This uncle had been living in New York for several years and his youngest child had been born there. Nachama was somewhat surprised at their way of living in a tenement on the east side of New York. She was shocked when she saw her aunt washing clothes. She was surprised that her aunt was not ashamed or embarrassed to be found doing such lowly drudgery. She gradually came to realize the relationship between the dignity of work and the right to hold up one's head as a free citizen.

She remembered her father once watching a big peasant boy carrying water into their home in Dworitz. Mordche Zisel had said: "We are in *gaulus* (exile) and Ivan carries water for us. Someday we shall be happy to carry our own water in a free land."

When Nachama reached her uncle's home, her cousins' first thought was to make her into an American girl immediately. They took her to a

She remembered her father saying: "Someday we shall be happy to carry our own water in a free land"

hairdresser to have her hair rearranged according to the fashion. They changed her name to Emma. This was not a correct translation of Nachama, which should have been Naomi, but they were influenced by the name of Emma Lazarus, whose poem, welcoming the oppressed to the new world, was inscribed in the Statue of Liberty. Nachama, an idealist of eighteen years, was easily persuaded to take the name of a woman like Emma Lazarus.

The prospect of education for everyone who wanted it was one of Nachama's most ardent reasons for coming to America and, years later, she often told her children that she had left her home and her parents in order to give them the glorious opportunity of being born on this side of the Atlantic Ocean.

She was very impressed when she saw a truck driver reading his newspaper. She wrote with enthusiasm to her parents, telling them that even laborers in America could read and write.

In spite of the urgings of her aunt and uncle that she rest from her long journey, Nachama, or Emma as she was now called, only a week after her arrival in New York, found work in an embroidery factory. She talked the forelady into hiring her although she knew nothing about using a sewing machine. She said she would learn, and she did. The first five dollars she earned was an excitement she would never forget, with the feeling it gave her of being free and her own mistress.

She attended the Education Alliance Night School, learned to read and write English, and studied American history and civics.

As soon as she was able, she began to read books in

English. She gradually read the English classics and she reread Tolstoy and other Russian classics in their English translations. Reading remained her chief pleasure throughout her long life.

While living in New York, she was always conscious of the fact that she was a young girl living in a large city without parents to guard her reputation. She was, therefore, very careful and associated only with her cousins, of whom she had many in New York.

Jacob was a friend of one of her male cousins. He was a young man of twenty-four, of medium height, dark complexioned with dark brown hair and eyes. He was pleasing in appearance and had a happy personality. Nachama met him many times with her cousins. One Sunday morning in early summer, he appeared at her door with a lunch box and asked her to go with him to Prospect Park in Brooklyn for a picnic. She hesitated for only a moment, and then accepted the invitation with pleasure.

Jacob proposed marriage to her that day; he knew if she were not prepared to accept him, she would not have accompanied him alone to Prospect Park. Such were the standards of 1895.

But Jacob had no special training, and times were not

Only a week after her arrival in New York, Nachama, renamed Emma, finds work in an embroidery factory

Jacob proposed marriage to Nachama that day in Prospect Park

good in New York. The doors of America were open to immigrants: they were given equal rights, free schooling and were not forced to do army service. But there was no organized way of helping them fit into the country and find jobs. Because of this, immigrants suffered great poverty during their early years.

Jacob found it difficult to earn enough to enable him to marry. He heard of a few Jewish men going to Canada, and after talking the matter over with Nachama, he decided to try his fortune in a less crowded area.

He traveled to Springhill, Nova Scotia, a small Canadian mining town where half a dozen Jewish men peddled necessities around the countryside. Springhill was far enough from a city of any size to make the peddler a welcome visitor. Only one Jewish family lived in the tiny town, and on Sunday the weary peddlers gathered in their home. This Sunday get-together was the one bright spot in their lonely lives.

The people in the area were poor and they bought only what they absolutely needed. Jacob peddled for two years, but was able to save very little money – not enough to go back and marry in New York. So he and Nachama finally decided she would come to Nova Scotia and they would be married there. In this way

they would spend less on traveling expenses. Jacob wrote his bride to bring from New York a trunk and a set of patterns for men's clothing. He had decided that peddling was not for him. He had other plans for the future.

Nachama traveled to Springhill with some newly-married cousins.

She and Jacob were happy to be together at last.

With high hopes they were married in Springhill in October, 1897. The legal ceremony was performed by the Protestant minister of this little community. He must have been touched by these two young people, almost penniless, speaking English with difficulty, brave enough to marry far from home, without even a clergyman of their own faith to perform the service. To satisfy their religious requirements, Jacob arranged for a friend with some religious education (he was also a peddler in the district) to read a Jewish marriage service for them. Attending the wedding were the cousins she had traveled with, the other peddlers and the one Jewish family that lived in Springhill.

The clerk in the hardware store where Nachama bought her few housekeeping wares had asked if he might come to the wedding. He was invited and he brought the gift of a china berry set, a large bowl and

twelve dessert saucers, which are still in use in my home.

Their first son was born in August of 1898. Jacob decided to give up peddling and move to a larger town.

Leaving his wife and baby in Springhill, he went to Saint John, New Brunswick, armed with the set of patterns which Nachama had brought to him from New York. He was lucky to get the support of the two largest clothing stores in Saint John and he started a small business manufacturing men's clothing. He rented a flat and sent for his wife and baby.

In time all the children of Sarah Elca and Mordche Zisel came to America. In 1901 Sarah Elca persuaded her husband to follow. Mordche Zisel got a job teaching in a New York *yeshiva*, but he was not happy and became ill. He longed to spend his last years in Palestine and to be buried in the ancient homeland beside Sarah Elca's father. Sarah Elca promised that if he recovered from his illness, she would go with him, although she was very reluctant to go so far from her family.

In 1905 they came to New Brunswick to see Nachama and her family before leaving for Palestine.

Jacob welcomes Nachama and their son to a new home

The following year Jacob bought a farm on the
outskirts of Saint John. There were by now three
more children. Each day Jacob traveled to his
business in Saint John, only five miles away but a
fifteen-minute trip by train. When he arrived home in
the evening, he changed into country clothes and
enjoyed doing the many chores of a farmer. He milked
his two cows, raised two calves which the children
named – one, Bossy, because she seemed aggressive
and the other, Pebble, because she was so tiny. He
read in a farm journal which he followed regularly
that if chickens had pleasant surroundings and music,
they laid more eggs. So he built a henhouse on high

ground with plenty of sun, and he sang to the chickens while he puttered around.

One evening in the late spring of 1909 Nachama sat under an apple tree while her children played around her. She watched Jacob digging in the vegetable garden. The smile on her lips was both amused and tender as she murmured, "My Tolstoy."

I remember that smile and that moment very well, for I was one of those children.

On their farm near Saint John, New Brunswick, Nachama watches
Jacob digging in the garden